Happy Hanukkah
        Benjamin and Joseph ♡ ♡
December 25, 2024
    We Love You So Much!

            Love, Shalom and G-D Bless.

            Poppi and Grandma
                Fuzzano

Hanukkah is Great!

By David and Betty Weinberger
Illustrated by Christine McParland.

Messianic Family Publishers
University Park, Illinois

Hanukkah is Great!

Messianic Family Publishers
553 Irving Place
University Park, IL 60484
www.amhehome.org

PRINTED IN THE UNITED STATES OF AMERICA.

Hanukkah is great because God is Great!

"Mom, Dad, I'm ready. When do you think we'll be leaving?" Anja* asked.

"Probably in 60 seconds or less," her father replied, as he raced down the stairs, grabbed his lunch box and headed for the door. Anja jumped out the door right after her father. Her mother followed, getting out her keys to lock the house.

"First we'll drop you off, "Anja's mother told her, "then I'll drive Dad to work."

"I sure wish my friend Catherine didn't have school today," Anja said. "I know she'd just love to go with me and help decorate the Weinbergers' house for Hanukkah."

The Weinbergers' house was where the big Hanukkah party took place each year.

"I'm sure she would," her father agreed. "But she can come over to our house any evening this week if she wants to celebrate Hanukkah with us."

*Anja is pronounced On'-yah.

When Anja saw the twins, Claire and Cara, at the Weinberger house, she forgot her disappointment that Catherine couldn't come. Then she saw Sarah! This sure was going to be a fun day!

The boxes with all the Hanukkah things were already on the floor in the living room. There were dreidels and lights and menorahs and books and tinsel.

Anja had celebrated Hanukkah for years, but it was always exciting to see the decorations again each year. And it was very special for the twins, because this would only be the second Hanukkah they celebrated.

As they decorated, they listened to Hanukkah music. The window decorations were looking very festive already, but when it got dark they would look even better. They got the lights up fast because Joel was home. He didn't even need a ladder! But he had to leave soon for his college classes and orchestra rehearsal.

As everyone admired the window Claire said, "Hanukkah is great!"

"I know," Anja said. "But Hanukkah is so great it's frustrating."

"What?!" Claire exclaimed.

"Well," Anja began, "it's frustrating because so many people don't even know about it, like Catherine. And they don't understand how jolly it is when you talk about it. School isn't out for Catherine. Joel has to go to college today. And Dad doesn't get the Hanukkah days off from his job, either."

"I know what you mean," Aunt Betty said. "It sure seems like we are a peculiar people, celebrating a holiday that not many people celebrate. But this actually helps us understand the real Hanukkah story better."

"What do you mean?" Anja and the twins asked.

S arah picked up a Hanukkah book and told the story.

"In Israel about two hundred years before Jesus was born, the Jewish people had a hard life. They were very peculiar, which means different, from the people around them. Israel was taken over by Syrian-Greek soldiers. They wanted the Jews to be like them and give up on God and the Bible.

"But the Jewish people devised a plan. Whenever they would meet to study the Scriptures, they would bring a dreidel along. If the enemy came by, they'd quickly hide their scrolls and pretend they were involved in a dreidel game."

"That was smart," Claire commented.

"Yes," Sarah said, "but there were some things that they just couldn't hide. If they refused to eat unclean foods or bow down to a false god, they were tortured or killed."

"So they had lots more reasons to be frustrated than we have," Cara said.

"Yes, their very lives were in danger," Sarah agreed. Then a godly man named Mattathias decided that he and his sons would fight against these enemies."

As Sarah turned the page, Claire exclaimed, "Wow, look at those elephants!"

"Yes, the enemy soldiers attacked with these huge elephants. And to make the elephants even more wild and dangerous, they fed them mulberry wine!"

"Oh no!" Cara said.

"But don't worry," Sarah continued. "Other men who loved God joined the small army of Mattathias and his sons. They bravely hammered away at the enemy wherever they saw them."

"That's why they were called the Maccabees," Anja remembered, "because Maccabee means hammer."

"And the Maccabees won!" Sarah exclaimed. "God helped them and that's why we can celebrate Hanukkah!"

"I thought Hanukkah was more about the miracle of the lights and not about winning a war," Claire said.

"Well, they're all connected," Sarah said. "Actually the word Hanukkah means dedication. After the war was won, the Jews took back their temple and wanted to re-dedicate it to God. But first they had to clean it. It was a big mess. The enemies put statues of their false gods in it. They killed a pig there and then boiled it and poured pig soup all over the temple."

Anja knew the rest of the story. "Once the temple was cleaned, they got ready to dedicate it. They poured purified oil into the great big menorah and lit it. But there was only enough oil for one day. To purify more oil would take eight days. They were sad because the lamp was always supposed to stay lit. Then, according to the legend which might really be true, a great miracle happened. "

"I know." Claire said with excitement. "When they went in with the new oil, the lamp was still lit! The one day's supply of oil lasted all the way till the new oil was ready. Eight days!"

"And that's why Hanukkah is celebrated for eight days with eight candles," Cara said.

Anja started smiling and said, "Well actually there are nine candles. But one of them doesn't count, because it's the servant candle. Eight days, nine candles. That could be a little confusing. "

Everyone laughed. Then a favorite Hanukkah song began…Oh Hanukkah, oh Hanukkah, come light the menorah. Let's have a party; we'll all dance the hora….

"Hey, why don't we all dance the hora,'" Cara said.

Joel's brother, Lael, just came back from the university library. Uh-oh, he had a feeling that he'd be roped into dancing the hora. Joel was all ready to leave, but he put down his violin case and joined in too.

"Hanukkah is great, isn't it?" Joel asked.

"Yes!" everyone shouted.

"Someone should tell that to Catherine!" Anja pleaded very loudly.

At Hanukkah people fry a lot of things in oil. This is a great reminder of the miracle of the oil in the lamp lasting for eight full days. Donuts (called soof-gahny-ote in Israel) and potato pancakes (called latkes) are traditional Hanukkah foods. On the third night of Hanukkah Anja's family celebrated by making a big batch of soof-gahny-ote. It turned out to be quite a "Joy-ful" event.

Anja and her mother had just finished sprinkling sugar and cinnamon on the warm donuts. Their dog Joy was being very obedient and just watching. Suddenly she sprang into action and stole a donut. Anja tried to catch her, but Joy escaped Anja's grasp. Joy ran back to the table and knocked three more donuts onto the floor.

"Dad!" Anja yelled.

Anja's father came in quickly and grabbed two donuts from off the floor. He lured Joy into the bedroom using them as bait. It was pretty funny. Anja even forgot her disappointment that Catherine couldn't come over because she had too much homework.

The fourth night of Hanukkah found Claire and Cara walking next door to the Weinbergers' house. They were delivering some Hanukkah cookies they just made.

Lael and Sarah were just getting out of the car and met the girls on the driveway. "Hi girls, want to come in?"

"No, we can't stay. We just wanted to bring you these cookies we made."

"Thanks a lot!" Lael and Sarah said.

Meanwhile, inside the house, Joel was asking where Lael was.

"He went to pick up Sarah," his father said. "She's having Hanukkah dinner with us tonight. Just think, by next Hanukkah, Lael and Sarah will be married!"

"That's an amazing thought," Joel said. "Hey, since Sarah will be here, we can all work on plans for the Hanukkah party coming up."

"Good idea," his mom agreed. "Do you have any ideas for the Hanukkah Man skit?" (An exciting skit with Lael dressed up as Hanukkah Man had become a fun tradition at the annual Hanukkah party.)

"Oh boy, do we have ideas!" Lael said as he and Sarah walked in. "And we also have ideas for dessert tonight! Cookies from Claire and Cara!"

The fourth night of Hanukkah was also very special at Anja's house. Catherine was planning to come over!

Anja finished wrapping her gift for Catherine. She quickly ate her dinner, then ran to the window and looked out. No Catherine. She joined her parents for a great dessert of homemade donuts. Then back to the window she ran. No Catherine. She played dreidel with her father. She looked out the window again. No Catherine. The phone rang. It was Catherine!

"Hi Anja," Catherine said. "I just got home now. The winter holiday party at the library lasted longer than usual. I'm so sorry I can't come over now. But I promise I'll go with you to the Hanukkah party."

"Really?" Anja asked, not knowing if she should get her hopes up.

"Yes, Anja, I promise. I really want to go."

Just then the doorbell rang. Claire and Cara and their family came to drop off some Hanukkah cookies. They stayed for two hours and played Scrabble and dreidel. They ate cookies and talked and laughed a whole lot. All three girls concluded, as they parted that night, that "Hanukkah is great!"

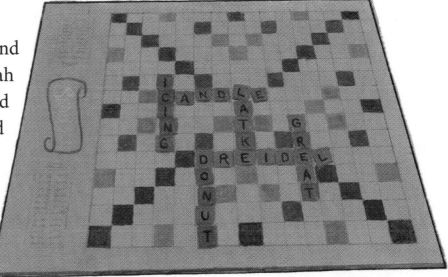

On the fifth night of Hanukkah there was a half-foot of snow on the ground. The menorah in the window looked so beautiful shining on the white snow. Anja loved the snow, even though it prevented Catherine from coming over to pick up her Hanukkah gift.

Because of the snow, Anja's swim meet was cancelled that evening. So Anja and her father used the evening to build a snowman. They came into the house rosy cheeked and ready for some hot chocolate.

Anja's mother just got off the phone. "They rescheduled the swim meet for tomorrow," she announced. "But I told them we couldn't make it because we'll be going to the Hanukkah party."

"Hurray for the Hanukkah party!" Anja shouted. "I don't mind missing the swim meet at all. The Hanukkah party is my favorite party of the whole year! OH NO!!"

"What happened?" Dad yelled as he rushed into the kitchen.

"OH NO!!" Anja said again. "Catherine's in the Park District Program too. She'll be going to the swim meet and will miss the Hanukkah party!"

It was the day of the Hanukkah party. At the Weinberger house, Hanukkah food that had been prepared days before was being reheated for the party. One hundred and fifty fried latkes were waiting for their turn in the oven.

Meanwhile, at Anja's house, the telephone was ringing. It was Catherine.

"Hi Anja. I'll be going to the party with you after all. My parents said that since I made a promise, I have to stick with it."

Anja was happy she was going, but also a little scared. Did Catherine really want to go or did she wish she could be at the swim meet? Would she be upset with Anja for inviting her?

"Oh well," Anja thought, as they left to pick up Catherine. "I'm happy to be going. And Claire and Cara will be there. And Sarah and Lael and Joel! And even Catherine will be there. Oh, why did the swim meet have to be scheduled for tonight?"

As they walked in, party noise was buzzing all throughout the house. A lot of happy conversations were going on at the same time. But when it came time to watch the old fashioned slide show about Hanukkah, things quieted down.

As a picture of a menorah appeared on the wall, Uncle David explained. "The Hanukkah menorah has eight regular candles on it. There's also one extra candle, taller than all the rest, in the middle. This is called the servant candle or Shamash in Hebrew. It's lit first so that it can then be used to light all the other candles for the evening.

"This servant candle reminds us of Yeshua (Jesus) who came to be a servant. And since this is the darkest time of the year, it's a great time to remember that Jesus is the Light of the world. Like it says in Isaiah 9, 'The people that walked in darkness have seen a great light.'"

Anja was wondering what Catherine was thinking about. She seemed very interested in the slide show, yet she looked a little sad. But when the slide show ended with a great Hanukkah song, Catherine chimed in with a happy voice, about the loudest in the room!

"Now it's time to light our Hanukkah menorah," Uncle David said. "Who would like the honor of lighting it?"

Several young people raised their hands, including Catherine.

"Please help Catherine be picked," Anja prayed quietly.

"Catherine, why don't you do it?" Uncle David said.

Catherine went up to the menorah with a huge smile on her face and a happy spring to her step. Her eyes were full of wonder and joy as the fire started to bounce from one candle to the next. But on her way back to her seat, she looked kind of sad.

Anja was not letting herself be too hopeful yet. Maybe Catherine liked being here, but maybe she didn't.

The food and fellowship followed. Anja saw Catherine take only one latke to start with. But then she went back and got three more, plus a kosher hot dog, some soup, and two homemade donuts (soof-gahny-ote).

Then Catherine and Anja joined Claire and Cara for a game of dreidel. They played three games, and Catherine never won, but she didn't seem to mind. She even seemed quite content to stick around, eat her donuts, and watch some of the younger children play. Aunt Betty gave everyone who played a bag of Hanukkah gelt (chocolate coins wrapped in gold foil).

The songs and the dances followed. Anja forgot to check on Catherine's reactions, because Anja herself was having such a good time.

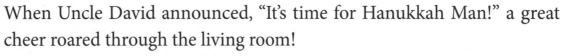

When Uncle David announced, "It's time for Hanukkah Man!" a great cheer roared through the living room!

L ael was dressed as "Hanukkah Man" and came down the stairs singing. *"Ho ho ho, hee, hee, hee, Happy Hanukkah from me to thee!"* Smiles and cheers broke out from the crowd.

Then Hanukkah man proceeded to tell the crowds about Hanukkah. He ended by giving a demonstration of how to make soof-gahny-ote.

"Here's the soft punchy dough that Sarah and I made earlier," Hanukkah Man explained. "I better punch it again to make sure…yep, nice and punchy. Can you hand me the oil, Sarah?"

"No, don't pour in the whole bottle!" Sarah exclaimed.

"Don't worry so much, Sarah," Hanukkah Man said in his low jolly-jolly voice. Amazingly it filled the pan to the brim without spilling over!

"Then we shape these into donuts and roll them in powdered sugar…"

"No Hanukkah Man!" Sarah tried to warn him. "Wait till the donuts are cooked to roll them in the sugar."

"Nonsense, why wait?" Hanukkah man said without waiting for an answer. "So then we drop them in the oil and …"

SPLASH! The donuts dropped in and there was a big explosion. There was fizz and spilling and bubbling over! All the children tried to get closer for a better look. What a show it was! The best one ever! Catherine had a smile on her face that didn't fade away.

Anja was encouraged that Catherine was still smiling. Finally Anja said, "Catherine, I've been trying to figure you out all evening. You're smiling now, but sometimes you looked sad and other times you looked happy. Do you like Hanukkah or not?"

"Oh Anja, Hanukkah is great!!" Catherine said very convincingly. "But it's so great, it's frustrating! I get so happy I'm here, and then I get sad that I missed all those other days of Hanukkah. You invited me over so many days, and I didn't come. You tried to tell me, but I didn't understand what a great holiday this is!"

"But Catherine," Anja said, "it's not over! There are still two more nights of Hanukkah. You can still come over to my house to celebrate."

"Really??? Hurray! Thank you, thank you, thank you!" Catherine said.

"And I still have a Hanukkah gift for you!" Anja added.

"Maybe you should give it to me when I come to your house tomorrow," Catherine said.

"No," Anja said. "You need to open this gift as soon as possible."

The doorbell rang and Catherine's father came to pick her up. As Catherine waved goodbye to everyone she yelled, "Hanukkah is great!"

"I know!" Anja joyfully agreed. "Don't forget to open your present right when you get home!" Anja's eyes were sparkling as she imagined the scene.

The End

Other children's books by the same authors:

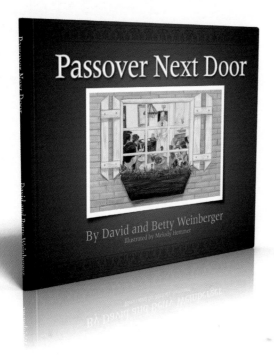

Passover Next Door

It's a holiday as old as Moses, and as current as today. So, come join Claire and Cara as they pay a visit next door and discover Passover! Feel the anticipation of the pre-Pesach preparation, the joy of the celebration, and the greatness of God's redemption celebrated in the Seder. Learn how the story of Passover points toward the Messiah, Yeshua (Jesus). And enjoy the family's object lessons of Passover that we discover along the way—matzo, charoset, horseradish, ravioli…Wait, did you say ravioli? Well, yes—you'll have to read the story to find out why! Parents and children alike will enjoy this vividly illustrated read-aloud.

Since I used to teach kindergarten, I love children's books. Your book is great—and so needed. I like the personal anecdotal aspect.

—Jamie Lash, Jewish Jewels Ministry, Ft. Lauderdale, Florida